D1165089

Copyright © 1984 American Greetings Corp. All rights reserved. Published in the United States by Parker Brothers, Division of CPG Products Corp.

Library of Congress Cataloging in Publication Data. Koenigsberg, Patricia Lakin. Fig Boot's Happy Day. Baby Strawberry Shortcake.
SUMMARY: Despite Fig Boot's forgetfulness, the birthday party for Baby Angel Cake goes off "berry" well.
[1. Birthdays—Fiction] I. Title
II. Series. PZ7.K818Fi 1984 [E] 83-22081 ISBN 0-910313-22-9
Manufactured in the United States of America 2 3 4 5 6 7 8 9 0

Baby Strawberry Shortcake

Fig Boot's Happy Day

Story by Patricia Lakin Koenigsberg
Pictures by John Gatie

Baby Strawberry Shortcake tossed back the covers of her fluffy quilt. She yawned a giant yawn. Then she rubbed her eyes and jumped out of bed.

"Yippee!" she shouted. "It's a sunny day. It's a wonderful day for Baby Angel Cake's birthday party. Baby Blueberry Muffin and I will plan a great party. It will be the best ever. We'll have cake and games and decorations and loads of presents."

Just then, Baby Strawberry looked out her window and noticed giant footprints near her garden. Then she heard a funny thumping sound coming from behind the leafy bush.

"Why it must be Fig Boot," said Baby Strawberry.

She called out, "Hello, Fig Boot. How are you this lovely morning?"

Fig Boot walked over to Baby Strawberry's window. He smiled a big, wide smile.

"You look as happy as I am," said Baby Strawberry.

Fig Boot nodded his head up and down.

Then Baby Strawberry got an idea.

"Fig Boot, could you help me?" she asked.

Fig Boot nodded eagerly.

"Please go to Baby Blueberry Muffin's house."

"Here is a note for her. It asks her to come here at three o'clock sharp. We will plan Baby Angel Cake's birthday party together."

"I wonder if I'm invited," thought Fig Boot.

"Don't look so sad, Fig Boot," said Baby Strawberry. "Everyone in Strawberryland is invited."

Fig Boot skipped happily over the hill. He headed for Baby Blueberry Muffin's house.

After a little way, he stopped and looked down into the valley.

"What a lovely view," thought Fig Boot. He just had to sit against a tree for a while. The birds in the trees sang beautiful songs. The frogs in the pond jumped long and far. And a rainbow painted a beautiful picture across the sky.

At the same time, Baby Raspberry Tart and her little monkey, Rhubarb, were walking along the path.

"Hello, Fig Boot. What are you doing here?" asked Baby Raspberry.

Fig Boot pointed to the beautiful view down in
the valley.

"You're right. It is lovely," said Baby Raspberry.
"Now I'm going to see Baby Angel Cake to wish her
happy birthday."

With that, Fig Boot jumped up. He had
forgotten about the message. He looked for the note
Baby Strawberry Shortcake had given him. Finally
he found it resting in the grass. He showed the note
to Baby Raspberry and Rhubarb. He pointed to
himself and then to the path that led to Baby
Blueberry Muffin's house.

"Oh! Are you in charge of delivering this message?" asked Baby Raspberry.

Fig Boot nodded proudly.

"Well, let's tie the note to this ribbon," said Baby Raspberry. She untied the red ribbon from her basket. "We'll tie the ribbon around your neck in a big, floppy bow so it will remind you to deliver your message."

Fig Boot tapped his tail politely to say thank you. They all waved good-bye.

Fig Boot continued along the path to Baby Blueberry Muffin's house.

After a little way, he heard a strange noise coming from the flower beds.

"What could that noise be?" thought Big Foot.

"It's me! It's me!" chuckled Baby Lime Chiffon. She crawled out from under a blueberry bush.

Fig Boot waved to his little friend.

"Play with me! Play with me!" pleaded Baby Lime Chiffon.

So Fig Boot and Baby Lime Chiffon curled
themselves into balls and rolled down the meadows.
Then they made chains of flowers for their heads.
Finally, they floated leaves at the edge of the
puddles made by the night's rain.

When they got tired, they lay down on the grass
and looked up at the sky. A group of beautiful
butterflies flew over their heads. One of them
circled around Baby Lime's face. Then it landed
right on Fig Boot's nose.

"They all know you," said Baby Lime Chiffon.
Fig Boot smiled and nodded yes.

He pointed to his friends, the butterflies, and
then to himself. Then he pointed over the hill.

"Are they your friends from Candy Canyon,
where you used to live?" asked Baby Lime Chiffon.

Fig Boot jumped up and down and danced around and nodded proudly, yes!

Suddenly, the note that Baby Raspberry Tart had tied with the red ribbon flipped up in Fig Boot's face.

Fig Boot remembered Baby Strawberry and the important job she had asked him to do. He *had* to deliver that message to Baby Blueberry Muffin!

"Oh, my! I hope I'm not too late," thought Fig Boot, as he quickly waved good-bye to Baby Lime Chiffon.

Fig Boot ran to Baby Blueberry Muffin's house
as fast as he could.

He knocked on her door. There was no answer.
He tapped on the window. There was still no
answer.

Fig Boot was very sad because he had missed
Baby Blueberry Muffin. He walked slowly back
along the path to Baby Strawberry Shortcake's house.

"Well, cheer up!" smiled Baby Strawberry.
"Blueberry came at three o'clock sharp anyway."

"Yes," interrupted Baby Blueberry Muffin. "It was
simple. I was daydreaming when I saw a whole
stream of butterflies in the sky. I followed them and
they led me all the way to Baby Strawberry's house."

And, sure enough, there
were all of Fig Boot's
butterfly friends from Candy
Canyon. They swirled around the room. Some
landed on Baby Strawberry Shortcake and Baby
Blueberry Muffin. Some landed on the streamers.

"They can come to the party, too," said Baby
Strawberry. "They make pretty decorations."

"And they are good, helping friends, too,"
thought Fig Boot. He was happy at last.

So, Baby Strawberry Shortcake and Baby Blueberry Muffin and Fig Boot finished getting ready for the party.

They put pink icing on the delicious white angel cake. Baby Strawberry Shortcake put a row of her best strawberries all around the cake.

They blew up balloons and made party hats for
Custard, Rhubarb, Cheesecake, and Souffle.

Then Baby Strawberry and Fig Boot worked
on a very special surprise for Baby Angel Cake.
It would come at the end of the party.

When all the kids had arrived, Baby Strawberry
said, "Let the party start!"

First, they all played musical chairs. Then, they all tooted their noisemakers and paraded around. The butterflies did their own special flying dance around Baby Angel Cake. She blew them kisses, bowed her head, and smiled her biggest smile!

Then Baby Angel Cake opened the brightly wrapped presents.

"Thank you for everything," said Baby Angel Cake, happily. "You are the best friends a girl could ever have."

Baby Strawberry said, "Let's give three cheers for Baby Angel Cake." Then she served everyone the cake.

"Delicious," said all the kids.

At the very end of the party, Baby Strawberry announced the special surprise she and Fig Boot had planned. They performed the song that Baby Strawberry Shortcake had written.

Fig Boot tapped his tail in tune while Baby
Strawberry sang:

We would all like to say,
Have a 'berry' happy day.
And when at last the party ends,
You'll have 'berry' many friends.

All the kids clapped. It was the best birthday
party ever!

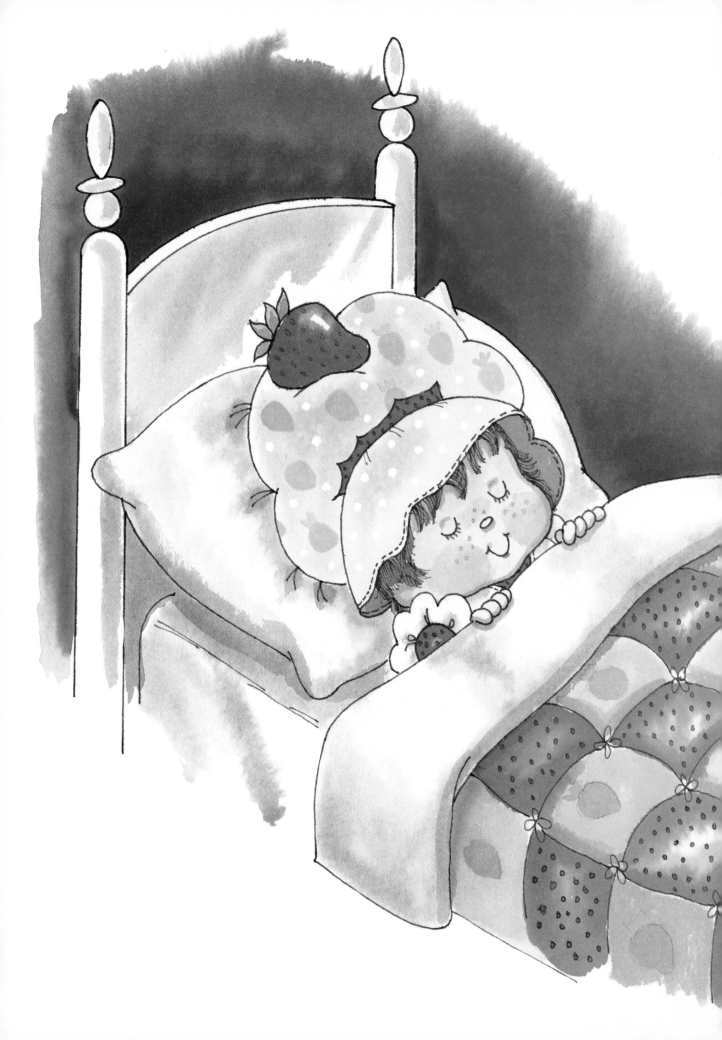

That night, when Baby Strawberry went to bed, she thought about the wonderful day she had. She nestled happily under her quilt and gave Custard an extra hug. Then she closed her eyes as she sang the special song:

We would all like to say,
Have a 'berry' happy day.
And when at last the party ends,
You'll have 'berry' many friends.